Still

Existing

A Compilation of Short Poems

By

Dominique Dorsey

Book Cover by Miblart

ISBN:9798864026557

First edition 2022

Table Of Contents

Introduction

Hello everyone! Welcome to the inside of my head. Where anything and everything is possible, and thoughts run a mile a minute. Firstly, I would just like to thank you all for picking up this book. My number one reason for writing this was so I wouldn't go completely insane with all these words, expressions, and emotions, staying bottled up inside. The second reason was you. I like to believe that all my experiences, whether good or bad, and my ability to express myself through writing is a gift to give to others to help them in their time of need. I want people to know that they are not alone in their emotions. Although situations may differ, the feelings conveyed through these poems are universal. At one point or another we all experience love, depression, confusion, and enlightenment. When I was going through things, I wrote about them. In that very moment I let all the words, tears, everything, just fall out onto whatever paper or notes in my phone. So, to my family who still sees me as an innocent little girl, please excuse the language on certain pages. To all my exes, friends, and loved ones, thank you for shaping me into who I am and for helping me write this book. To all my readers, live to fight another day.

The Hard Times: Everything In Between

Fresh Air

I get it
I really do
And I'm not blaming you
Everyone is entitled to their feelings
But it hurts when you lash out at me
The person who has your best interest at heart
The person who is always holding you down
The person who got your back with no hesitation
And at times like this
It's like what am I doing it for
Why must I put up with the bullshit
The tiny stabs
The little daggers
It hurts
I'm not bleeding
But I don't have to be
I feel it
From someone I trust
Someone I love
And I understand misery loves company
But must I endure your pain too
Must I hold my breath while you're being dragged under
Is that what it means to be there for you
Or when you slip under
Cuz it happens to everyone
Will you let me stay on dry land
And pull you up with me
Cuz that's where we belong
That's what friends should do
I love you seriously
And I don't want to lose you
But I don't want to tolerate your abuse for the sake of love

I don't want to be dragged through the mud every time you lose your
footing
We both deserve fresh air
And I will never take away yours
So don't take away mine

I Reached for You

I'm standing there
Watching you
As you're being taken further and further away from me
We used to be in the same place
Playing
Goofing around
Chilling
Living
It was calm then
The waves rocking calmly
The noise nothing above a whisper
The breeze ever so soft against our skin
It was calm then
Until it wasn't
And the waves got bigger
And the noise grew a bit louder
And the soft breeze got a lil chill in it
So we stood a bit stronger
Tuned out the noise
Shook off the chills
And we still had each other
And it didn't last
And it was calm again
Until it wasn't
And a wave came so big
Knocked us right off our feet
Got so loud that we felt like lions were roaring in our ears
And the breeze felt more like a hurricane
And we tried
We tried hard
And my foot found the bottom
And I stood up
Braced my body against the blows
Ignored the screaming

Sought shelter in my happy places and positive pass times
And I reached for you
And you threw driftwood at me
I reached for you
And you succumbed to the lions
I reached for you
And you told me that the hurricane already ripped you apart
I told you stand up
Just get up
Fight it
You can do it
And I reached for you
And you didn't respond
I reached for you
And you were giving yourself away
I reached for you
And you thought of ending it all
So I jumped back in
Determined to help you in any way I could
Focused on pulling you out
Praying that we'll both have the strength and courage to make it through
But I'm watching you
And you're not putting your feet down
You're not holding on to me
You're floating in the opposite direction
And then I start to sink
And as I'm holding my breath trying to pull you up
I run out of oxygen
And as much as I don't want to
I choose to come up and breathe
I stand up
And as I'm standing there
Watching you
As your being taken further and further away from me
I realize you have to want it too
And fight for it with everything you have
And I watch you rising and falling with the waves

Letting the wind take you in any way it desires
Singing along to the noise

Can't Compute

All I want to do is make it right
Make it feel right again
Make us right again
I'm counting down the minutes till I hear your voice again
Get a text from you
Any indication of existing
Every minute feels like hours in agony
I can't function fully
Properly
Till we work things out
My mind is only half occupied with failed means of distractions
I want you
This hole of darkness is growing bigger the longer we're like this
You feel galaxies away from me right now
I feel more broken than usual
And the longer we wait
The bigger my insecurity monster gets
The harder it is to fight
All I ever need is someone who is willing to show up for me
Always
No matter how difficult, how lazy, how unwanting, or tired
Just show up
Be there
Consistently
That's the goal
That's love
That's the struggle
And no one is ever willing
Not yet anyways
I'm scared

One-Way Track

I hope I'm not losing you
And this may sound silly to say
But it frightens me
Deeper than my darkest fear
Realer than any emotion I ever felt
Because at least those could be dwindled down and managed
Cuz I can get through anything with you
And I know you will protect me
But if you weren't there
I feel like it would be equivalent to hundreds of unopened closet doors
Harboring the wildest and inexplicable horrors an imagination can
conjure
I would much rather be on a plane with turbulence
Then for you to lose sight of our future together
I've grown to hate the monotone question of "how was your day"
Because I know after this there's no more till the next day
With the same question
Till the next day
With the same question
But I am trying to appreciate it
And cherish it
Since it's all I have to hold on to now
Till the next day
All I have to look forward to
And at least it's something
At least it's a pinhole of proof that you still care about me
I don't want to lose you
Cuz you say your mind is on a one-way track right now
But I know that track doesn't include me
There is no passenger seat
There is no wingman
There is no trusty sidekick
It's just you
And how can we build together

If you're already building by yourself
And not willing to share the blueprints
How do I know
That your mind will ever come off this one track
Or that you'll finally turn around and see that you left me
How far do you have to go
And will you be back for me
Because I'm tired of feeling forgotten about
I'm tired of feeling ignored
I'm tired of feeling like I'm a nuisance
And doubting myself
Your mind is on a one-way track
And my mind is lost without you
Staring at your railroad to your future
Sitting in the dust
Writing our names with my pointer finger
Encasing it in a heart
Listening to your faint hum in the distance
Wishing for the day it grows louder
Don't leave me
I whisper to myself
Already knowing how desperate I must sound
Don't leave me

Lessons Pt. 2

And there have been guys in which I had nothing in common
And despite how good they looked
And how much they wanted me
I said no
Because it didn't feel right
And I'm not tryna force anything
With anybody
Just to be in a relationship
I'm not eager to find a boyfriend
I'm so good with being single
Unless I'm horny
But I can't just have casual sex
It doesn't work for me
I'm not one of those types of people
I wish
I wish I could care less sometimes
But I'm happy that I don't give in to my urges
And it's not like I go after bad guys
Or the thrill of someone
Or dating all these fuckboys
I have high standards
And I'm very, very, very selective
So it's not like I'm just throwing my love around
Just handing out pieces to my heart
Cuz that's dumb
I barely let people touch me or stand close to me
My guard is always up
I am very protective of myself
I dead people really quick
And get turned off really quick
And I don't forgive people
I don't have any issue with walking away
One of my strengths and my weaknesses
I know what I deserve, and I will not settle for less

And I know when to say no
And yet I'm here
After I done made you special
Accepting all your red flags and filing them under "Nobody's Perfect"

Your So-Called Love

You told me you're selfish
That you're not thinking about me
That you're unhappy
That you're always gonna look out for yourself first
So where does that leave me
And you say you don't know how to answer that
That I need to be clearer in what I'm trying to ask
And all I want to know is where do I fit in to your little agenda
When you're bored
When you don't want to be alone
When you want something to fuck
What do I mean to you
If you claim you feel what you always felt about me from day 1
And it's going on almost 2 years
Are the same and only feelings you felt from me when we were still
figuring shit out
Before we went through all our shit
Before we were even official
And I tell you I think you're not capable of loving me
And you nod your head
You don't disagree
You don't reassure me or comfort me
You let me walk away
Crying
While you stare at your phone and watch your movie
Cuz obviously my feelings aren't as important as the plot of the story
Saying I'm coming out of my face
And I'm crying over nothing
Really
And I'm supposed to think you love me
Hehe yeah
That's love alright
Never once uttered it purposely
But you loving me

You don't even kiss me
But you loving me right
Yep
Thanks
Fuck you
And fuck your so-called love

Strong Too Long

I just need a little comforting
Right now
A joke
A compliment
A distraction
I just need something
To forget
I need a moment to cry
And be weak
Because I've been the strong one for too long
The one that always puts a smile on people's faces
To hold everything together
To merge between the two
I need my peace
And you bring me that
That comfort I always mention
That soothing richness I get filled with
I just want to forget
And not feel
And just go
I wish I could do more
I wish I could take away the pain
I wish I could stop sobbing
I'll be alright
I am alright
I just need a moment
To breathe
And clear my mind
Hopefully
I'll be alright

Straw, Sticks, or Bricks

You think you can do me a solid
And stay solid
When the rain turns the dirt to mud
When the ocean sweeps the shore away
Can you stand behind your word
Can you look me in my face
Will you lie all my fears away
Or tell the truth if it caused me pain

Portrait Bust

I wanted you to see me
I wanted you to value me
To realize I wasn't just a shiny object
Amusing for a time
And able to dispose of later
I wanted you to know me
Know that I don't complicate things
Know that I understand
Know that I'm considerate and kind and giving
Always
To you
For you
Always
I wanted you to believe in me
the best in me
About me
I wanted you to get me
Have faith that I will choose the right choice
I wanted you to include me
Even as little as possible
The smallest of amounts would have meant gigantic figures
Did I want too much?
I'm not sure yet
But I won't settle for less
I won't accept anything less
You can't tell me how to feel
And if I'm hurting you can't try and put me in my place
You can't turn us off and on like a switch
You can't mold me into your pedestal figurine
"Your queen"
I am already fully figured in my own design
I have cracks
I have chipped pieces
I have pieces that I'm still working to glue back on

And I have pieces that make me lighter since it's fallen
But majority of me is there
Standing
And you can admire my work
You can help with some repairs
And you can do some damage
And none of them are ever choices
They just happen
So be careful
I'm fragile

Sleepy Baby

People who want the benefits of a relationship
Without actually being in a relationship
Is the exact equivalent to a baby who's fighting sleep
Shhh
It's ok
You're not gonna miss out on anything
You're tired
Go to sleep

Lessons Pt. 3

I'm sorry that I feel like you compliment me
And I know your heart is big like mine
So I'm sorry that I wasn't hurt like you
To close myself off so deeply
I'm sorry that I'm hesitant sometimes
Because like you
I don't want to be hurt again
And I feel like everything falls into place sometimes so perfectly
That it's hard not to move forward
I'm sorry that I don't know how to act before a relationship
I don't know what I'm supposed to be doing
I feel like I have a general understanding of who you are
More than a general understanding
And our vibes click
You get me
And I see that
I appreciate that
And this is not just how I'm acting before a relationship
This is me
This is how I will be
You're not gonna get any less than this
And you've earned it
You didn't freak out
You calmed me down
You didn't think any less of me
You say it's because you're understanding
But that's huge
That says a lot
And you stayed on the phone with me even though I wanted to hang up
because you thought that's what I needed
And it was
You admitting when you're wrong
That's earning it
It's not easy for people to do that

And apologize for it
Even though I didn't forgive you in that moment
But you worked and showed me that I mean something to you
The random phone calls
Answering my texts
Falling asleep with me on the phone
That all means something
People don't just do that
So I'm sorry you feel like I care about you too much
I'm sorry I show my appreciation more than you think I should
I'm sorry I can't control my feelings for you
I'm sorry that I think we should give us a try
I'm sorry

Lessons Pt.1

I'm sorry that I live in a world where too much love is a problem
I love myself
So much so that I have enough left over to share with others
And I do not love everyone
I don't even like most people
Because yes not everyone is deserving
And I know that
Like the last guy I was talking to
I did not love him
I could not love him
I didn't want to love him
Because he wouldn't appreciate the beauty in me
Not that he was a bad person
He just didn't know how
And so it was nothing serious
And easy to let go
And not get attached
And I understood that
My first love was kind of an asshole
He didn't understand how I could love him
Since he hadn't accomplished anything yet
And he felt like less of a person
Because of it
And he could not love me
Because he did not love himself
I learned not to go for the first person that shows interest in me
I learned what it felt like to be alone with someone
I learned what being stood up felt like
And what I would stand for when I'm with someone
I learned that loving someone was the most beautiful and hurtful thing
that could happen
I learned that people will say anything to make you do as they want
I learned people can be selfish
And I took my time and I healed

And then there was my second love
And he was everything the first was not
He was kind
And beautiful
And patient
And he showed me in every way possible
That he cared
And supported me
And I reciprocated the feeling
It was the one time that I ever felt equal
Like we were on the same page
Same feelings
And then he got evicted
And was homeless
And had to work two jobs
And still go to school
And I waited
Because he showed me he was worth it
But he blocked me out
And forgot about me
And I understood
Because that would be a lot for any person to handle
So I understood if he needed to figure things out
Even if he didn't voice it
But he got a system together
That worked for him
And was working through it
And somehow decided that he didn't have time for me
Or wanted to make time for me
But had time for his fans
And his friends
And his followers and subscribers
And I couldn't allow myself to tolerate his treatment anymore
And I realized that everything probably wasn't real for him
Like it was for me
But I learned that some things are just temporary
We meet people and are put in people's lives for a reason

And that's it
And once again I accepted it
So when you came along
Your flirting words didn't take me
The compliments didn't make me think of more
The way you looked at me didn't entrance me
It was the fact of you being there for me
When I was scared
When I was embarrassed
When it mattered
And not leaving
The way you carried yourself
Your maturity
Our conversations
That's what did it

Lessons Pt. 4

You know how you have a movie
It's not your favorite movie in the world
But it's a pretty good movie
And you put it on every once in a while
And you still enjoy it
And then one day you can't find it
But it's like ehh no worries
Because you know it's somewhere
And there's other things to do
And then time passes
And then you find the movie but it is all scratched up and bent and you
don't know if it will play again
And that feeling of shock and sadness and willing for everything to be
okay kinda makes you want to watch the movie even more
Or think about the next time you can see it
Or that it just might be in your top 5 favorite movies in the world
Well that's what happened
That's exactly what happened
But you're the movie
Like if the movie were fine and I found it in perfect condition it would
have been fine
But since it wasn't it made the value go up
Because now there was a chance of losing it
A chance of me losing you
And me praying for you
And worrying about you
And thinking about you
Just made me care about you more

Lessons Pt. 5

I tried to back off
I tried to give you space
Trust me when I say
I tried to take things slow
But I feel like your actions are not taking it slow with me
The only thing you're slow with is saying you're committed to me
Because you tell me that you're not interested in anyone else
So you basically already are
And I don't know what else you're not doing now
That you would be doing if we were together
I mean you are the one saying things like
"When you're my wife"
And seeing us with no kids
And talking about a far, far future
That's not taking it slow
That doesn't make me feel like we're taking it slow
And how am I just supposed to be normal with that
Or not be attached to you
I just don't understand
And yes everything is fine
Nothing is wrong
But this isn't the first time this has come up
And I'm only addressing it because it still bothers me
I thought we were going somewhere
That you were maybe catching up
That's all
But if you still want me to slow down
I'll try

Leave A Message

Please leave your message at the tone:
Beep
So I'm sorry to be calling you
I know this is not what you want to hear
I know you're mad at me
I know that I love you and that's messing everything up
Because what we had was supposed to be a non-committed thing
Something more of a social gathering
Or a late-night house trip
Whatever voids needed to be filled actually
Everything in terms
Accept using that word
Cuz for some reason that word is too heavy
All the baggage packed in it
Too much responsibility
Too much creativity
Too much longevity
I'm sorry for calling
I don't even know what I'm saying
I miss you
And I wish there were a better way
I don't know what to do
I know you care about me
The way you make me feel says that
The smile I put on your face
I know it's real
All the time we spent together
You are everything I ever wanted
And that's why it hurts so bad
That you're everything I can't have
So I'm gonna go
And I hope I didn't just walk out on the best thing that ever happened to
me
That I didn't have enough faith in you

That your actions supersede your words
I hope I'm making the right choice of letting you go
Escaping my love's blindness
Ending our beautiful journey here
Before it ever really began
With a test run like that though
I don't see how we couldn't make it
But with you as my dealer promising me there's no more road ahead
I hope you understand why I have to stop
I can't be down for the both of us
I can't love me for the both of us
I'm sorry
Click.

The Good Times: Being In Love

Caged Bird

It sits there
Heavy
Burdening
Ugly
Unwanted
Caged Away
Looking forward still
To the day it can be released
 And who knows if it can fly
It only knew life in captivity
Eating away at its own feathers
Chirping away at possibilities
It is inconvenient
A fool's errand
Dumb
But still it only manages to think about trying
About one day maybe flying
Maybe opening the gate
Maybe not being restrained
Is there any right time to go
Because there's no turning back
It can't be unspoken
Wait
Don't set it free
It's caged for a reason
What if he can't say it in return

Bermuda

So picture this
You've been dreaming about going to Bermuda your whole life
You save up
You book a flight
You go
You get the hotel room where the doors slide right on open to the beach
And you're entranced by the beautiful view
The water glistening
Clearest of blues
The sun reflecting its angelic light off every wave
Sparkling off every corner
Twinkling off every curve
The sand
The perfect combination of risings and fallings
Ups and downs
Smooth and bumpy
And yet
It is still sand
It is still one cohesive structure that forms the shore
And as you are gazing through the glass pane of the door
A tear swells in your eye
Fore you have never seen a sight so simply astonishing
You open it
A gust of wind skillfully carries the smell of happiness and delight to
bless your airways
You inhale deeply as you close your eyes
You don't step yet
But you imagine the feeling of the sand
Under
Over
And in between your toes
The soft crunching sound it would make
The heat that would radiate off it
You open your eyes

And you're still in the doorway
Why haven't you moved yet
Why aren't you running around letting the tiny tan particles kick up
behind you
Why aren't you splashing in that iridescent water
You're standing there unable to understand your hesitation
This is all you ever wanted
You are finally here
What's the hold up
And then you realize
You haven't put on your bathing suit yet

Ne-Yo

I would never want to rush you
But honestly
I can't grasp why we are not together
I mean what more can I do
To show you
Prove to you
Why am I still not good enough
What am I lacking
Why can't you trust me
To not make the same mistakes your ex did
Why don't you have faith in me
That this is who I am
And this is who I will be
Believe in me baby
That I will do right by both of us
That we are winning as long as we have each other
I'm not going anywhere
(besides the occasional trip to Florida)
I'm always gonna want you
And want us
When will the previews be enough
And the real movie begins
Do you still feel like you don't know me well enough
I've told you everything you need to know about me
You see what kind of person I am
Plus the way we feel about each other
There's no reason to be apart any longer
No reason that we shouldn't be claiming each other
Cuz at this point in time
Regardless of titles
I am yours
And you are mine
You tell me everything
And I tell you everything

What you lack I will provide
And what I lack you will provide
We already built a foundation
Of love, trust, and open communication
When will we finally move in
And start living what we created
Baby all I'm saying is
I want to be yours already
Cuz no one has and no one will
Love you the way I do
So let me love you

When It Happened

You know you ask yourself all the time
In preparation
Cuz you know it's bound to come up
And you think really hard
And try to recall
And really remember
When you knew you fell in love
When you realized your heart was no longer your own
That somehow you recovered from all the falls you took
And you're ready to leap again
And you ask yourself
When did it all change
When no one else started to matter
Because your mind was on him
And only him
And you saw no one else
Because your eyes found something in his
And only his
And you think back to that day
When you happened to see him for the very first time
And I really mean very first
It was normal
Like any other moment
And then the moments after
Like right after
There was a little question in the air
A little curiosity, some familiarity
But there was comfort
A calmness
A look that said everything is gonna be okay
And it was
And then you think back to the days when you missed him so much
That you thought your body was gonna burst
That your heart ached

That every second ticked by slower than the last
When you thought you had found a cure
A healing power
Happiness
And it was gone
So abruptly
Like life itself
And the only way to cope with your loss
Was through poetry
Words dancing across the page
Singing your passion and pain
Tasting your thoughts and dreams
The wishes you had wished
The endless bargains that were single handedly made
All the prayers
All the could've beens and what ifs
And as you let your words flow on the blank lines ahead
Pouring out your soul amongst deaf ears
That's when it hit you
Because why else would you care so damn much
Why would it pierce through your flesh like a carver's knife to butter
Why would it leave you thinking all day and all night
Why would it have you permanently stuck in a euphoric temple of
memories
Reminiscent on the way he looks at you
The way he touches you
Gentle
Sweet
Knowledgeable of your body
Aware of how his fingerprints lay resting on your skin
It was then
In solace
Writing to you
Writing to God
Writing now
That I knew I fell in love
That everything was so right for a reason

That the calm was forever calming
That my smiles were the brightest with you
That I could be the best version of myself and you could accept that
And be there
My laughter genuine
My mind controlled
Programmed to everything involving you
Although it is not the right timing or place to say anything about it
That even though there never is
Courage doesn't stand before you
Eagerly waiting to see what's behind door number two
Because one is always disappointment
And three is always the best
But three is a long way from here
And two is every other option in the blue
The only place those words exist
Is on this page
Patiently waiting
To be spoken out loud
To hear it come out my mouth
Dare it to be written
I love you

That Fire

You ignite a fire in me
So hot
I don't ever see it ever extinguishing
The red and orange and blue hues of our flame
Representing the known, unknown and what doesn't need to be known

The Best Love Story

******

You changed my world
Yes
My whole world
You make life worth living again
Like everything has a purpose
A meaning
A rhyme
In the sense where a word at the end of the sentence
Corresponds with another word at the end of the next sentence
And baby
We spent our life before going through whatever we had to go through
To get to the end of our sentence
And the way we rhyme
The way our minds are similar but yet so diverse
The way our bodies constantly fuse together like magnets
The way you look at me
And I to you
How comfortable we are
How you feel so familiar to me
It's only been two months since we met
And here we are
Every curve of you matching with every curve of me
Everything falling into place
Feeling so beautiful
So right
So special
We rhyme
Like the test of time
So divine
You were written to be mine
In all our glory
The best love story
Of how Nikki and ******

Conquered everything that went askew
You're amazing
And I'm so happy you're in my life
Happy Thanksgiving

****** = Name has been omitted

Blue Skies

It's amazing how
I can love you so much
How the simple touch of my fingertips to your skin
Can make all my insides turn to jelly
And for some reason
I just wanna cry
The overwhelming sensation
Of you
Being mine to love fully
To share myself with completely
To undoubtedly commit to
I get lost within you
Not in a sense where I lose sight of myself and what I want
But me being so deeply involved and curious
Me exploring your moods
Emotions
Your thoughts
Being a part of your daily routines
Your life
Me knowing you on a whole new level
Turning corners to hallways that leads to your darkest secrets
Stairways that lead to your highest aspirations
Rooms filled with endless banter of celebrity gossip that you'll one day
be a part of
And many more that discuss the simple joys of what's for dinner tonight
and how was your day
My love for you is so fulfilling
That every obstacle that I'm faced with
Is not an obstacle at all
Just a passing rain cloud in the bluest, clearest sky on a perfectly
weathered day

The One He Never Heard

I'm sitting here trying to figure out what I should say
What I haven't said yet
How many other ways can I tell you I love you
How many times can I tell you your time is precious to me and all I want to do
is make you happy
How else can I explain the depth of our connection
And the many emotions you make me feel
I honestly don't know
I hope I tell you often enough that I appreciate you
That I'm thankful for your existence
I try and make it a point to express that
So you never feel like I'm taking you for granted
So on this Valentine's Day
I have nothing new to say to you
But I promise to keep saying it
I promise to continue living my life showing you that I'm not just saying words
because they sound nice
I mean it all
Every time
I promise to keep the foot rubs coming
Promise to keep the good food cooking
The sexy lingerie wearing,
Suck on your dick at night having,
Sending you nudes at work playing vibes I give you just because
Promise to keep my moods and temper tantrums to a minimum
Promise to think of new ways to build us up
Support you
Comfort you
Be there for you
Ride for you
I promise to bother you when you had a boring day
And try and make you smile when you had a rough one
I promise to continue to give you my all
Continue to grow with you
Continue to be by your side
Because you're stuck with me now
Happy 1st Valentine my love

To Growing Gray

I love you
From the way you look at me
To your corny jokes
Escaping from your beautiful bright big smile
Your lips
Pleasuring my mind, body, and soul
To your fingertips
Intertwining with mine
Your acceptance and surrender to my touch
Receiving my energy
Reciprocating and sharing your own
Your body sculpted by hard work, determination, and divine lineage
Your childish ways
That's just a reminder that it's okay to have fun
To live
To laugh
I was crying in the car because it had just hit me
This was the moment
This is the day
A part of me is scared
There's no place I wouldn't go
No place I'd rather stay
I trust you with all of me
Always
Whatever you say I'd do
You could lead me down a foreign path
 I'll follow
Tell me to take a leap of faith and I'll dive
And being that powerless
Being that vulnerable
Is frightening
But I believe in you anyway
I believe in us
And this

Anyway
I know my heart is strong cuz it has the capacity to bounce back
To love like you've never been hurt before
Never been broken before
It's not as easy as it may seem
But it's always been in me
Because if I loved them
All while being the wrong one for me
Imagine the endless possibilities
Of loving the right one
The mountains we can move
The world trembling at our feet
Leaving you is always the hardest and worst part of my day
And that tells me from now
I'm not supposed to
So here's to growing together
Growing closer
Growing wiser
And growing gray

Thankful for 2004

So yesterday was Thanksgiving
And even though holidays are supremely hard for me
This one was one to cherish
And on a day to share what I am most grateful for
I didn't have the courage to express my feelings in person
So without further ado
I am thankful for you
In all ways I can fathom
I am thankful for the way you look at me
Geez how I feel like you're seeing my soul
And accepting me
I am thankful for your patience
Cuz I can do the most sometimes
And you understand
And comfort me
I am thankful for your amazing mind
And your level of capability to understand me
Cuz for a long time I feel like people didn't
Except for my friends
And I never was good at communicating or talking
But somehow you get me without saying a word
And when you don't you ask me
And ask again
And ask a third time cuz I'm stubborn and still figuring out how to form
it into words
I am thankful for your heart
For letting me in
And caring
And trusting me with it
And giving me a chance
I am thankful for your drive
That inspires me to never give up
And be responsible
And think ahead

And make the right choices
I am thankful most of all for your presence
And I probably say this a lot
But your company means so much to me
Your time so valuable
And the moments we spend together
Even just sitting on the couch watching a terrible movie
Or riding the trains home
Matter
That time matters
I am thankful babe
For all you are
And all you do
And I'm thankful for being your girl
Finally

Rider

I still get butterflies when I see you
When I look at you too long
When I feel you
I still see my future in your eyes
In your words
In your plans for us
I still see why I was never able to leave you alone
Why I always wanted you
You are amazing
And quite nonchalant or clueless about how amazing you are
I try and embrace and hold on to the moments that I'm with you
Cuz even when I'm with you I miss you for the times you're not gonna be there
When I have to go home
When I go away
And that's me worrying about things that haven't come to fruition yet
Which doesn't make sense
So I focus myself back into the moment
Moments of me being on your couch
Moments of you having your arms around me
Moments of our bodies connecting
Moments of us
I love it
And sometimes I feel like if I hold on too tight
I'll end up pushing you away
But then you'll say something like "Good. Cuz you're stuck with me"
And I just think to myself like yeahhh you don't even know that YOU'RE actually stuck with ME
You can talk for days
And I'll always listen
You can ask me to tend to your needs
They'll be taking care of
Rub your feet
I gotchu

Hold you down
Try and stop me
Watch your back
I won't look away
You don't even realize yet how much of a rider I actually am
But that's okay
Cuz what's forever doesn't worry about time
And you my dear are all mine

<u>You</u>

My every breath is you
Loving you
Thinking of you
Worrying about you

I Love Love

Man I love being in love
This probably is the longest chapter in my book
I love the words pouring out of me
Expressing how I feel about you
How I dream about you
Fantasize
Romanticize
The words flow like water reaching a cliff
As beautiful as the resulting fall
Freeing
It makes me feel lighter
Happier
Just thinking about it
Being able to process and gather my thoughts into a solidified form
Releasing
Describing your beauty
Emphasizing what I cherish most about you
How euphoric I feel
So wonderful
And when I start to rhyme
Boyyyy it's about that time
Cuz the corniness and cheesy
Can make anyone queasy
Cuz I be laying it on thick
And it's not even always about your …
I just be getting in the zone
Writing the words to my moans
I love love
Got me feeling like a dove
Ha
I'm done being silly
I just love love

Fulfillment

There's nothing you don't do
And it's crazy to me
That somehow you know the unknown
The unspoken
And you just act on it
I needed attention
I felt myself yearning for reassurance
I'm not perfect
And this I feel is one of my flaws
So I don't speak on it much
I didn't this time
I just let my crazy pass
As I usually put it
And without any insinuation
You showed me exactly what I was looking for
Exactly what I wanted
Exactly what I needed
Thank you
Thank you for the little things that I adore and thrive on so much
Thank you for thinking of me
Thank you for being you
I appreciate you to my fullest capabilities
And I'll spend every day showing you how much I do
I can say I've never experienced a love like this
Every part of me belongs to you
And not just focusing on the physical possession aspect of it
But every part of me holds so much love for you
It's as if you are in me
As much as my mind holds the thought of you
My heart holds my will for you
My fingertips, the touch of you
My ears, the sound of you
And so on and so forth

You are as much a part of me as I am in my life
And I couldn't have given myself to a better person

You Give Me

You are the best part of my day
One text from you can still send me over the moon
You are the person who I want to tell everything to first
You make my soul smile
I can feel the warmth my body stirs up when I think of you
When I touch you
Your body comforts me in a way that no one else can
The way you care about me and love me makes me get emotional
Knowing that you think of me too
And want to know what I'm doing or how I'm doing
When you are inside of me
Giving me all of you
Filling me like a candlelight in a small dark cave
My moans unable to be ceased
Your motion unable to be stilled
Us enjoying us
And when we both have shared ourselves so much and I feel the love
coasting back and forth between our bodies
Surrounding us
Encasing us
The little kisses
The passionate grabbing
Gripping on to my body as if I'm oxygen and you're on your last breath
When everything is just right
And I know there's no other place or no other person or no other time or
no other dimension I would rather be in this moment with
I have nothing else to surrender but my tears
So I cry
I am weak
I am vulnerable
I am longing to stay
Longing to remember this feeling
Not only in this moment but this part of our lives
Together

Replay

We're standing there
Holding hands
Gazing lovingly into each other's eyes
Our family filling the room
Going before God
Eagerly wanting to start our lives together

Love Me

Love me
For the person I am
For the person I've been to you
For the person I'm learning and choosing to be
Love me
When I make you happy
But even more so when I make you mad
When the world seems to be crumbling
When time feels like it's at its end
Love me
Love me when I'm scared
Love me when I'm hurting
Love me when I'm being a pain in your ass
Love me when I make mistakes
Love me when I feel alone
Love me when I don't know how to explain what I feel
Love me when I'm trying
Love me when I'm giving you all that I have to give
And when your love is the only thing I have to hold on to
I will know the definition of true love

The Bad Times: Break Ups

Here's Hoping

I want you to know
You deserve love
You deserve a light that brightens up your day
You deserve the best this world has to offer
Even though you've done wrong
There's so many things you've done right
Do not punish yourself for the things you can't control
Do not punish yourself for keeping your head above water
You are a good man
You are fighting for survival in a system designed to fail you
You are enough
You are divinely made
And although I may not be what you want
Or what you need
You will forever be in my heart
And I will always want the absolute best for you
You showed me a side of you that was so amazing and genuine
I don't know if I'll ever be able to let that go
But I will give you your time
I understand although I may want to
I can't fix all your problems
I can't save you
What I can do
I will always be here for you
Whether you decide to come back to me or not
I don't see this as the end for us
Don't lose yourself
Don't lose sight of all the things you can still accomplish in the world
You are great
You are appreciated
For everything you've ever done for me
Through the happiness and the pain
I have grown and learned so much
I still and always will love you

And even though I'll learn to live without you
And not need you
I will always want you

I Thought A Lot

I thought you knew me
I thought you understood who I was
As a person
As a soul
As a gift
I thought we clicked
Like no other
Matched deeper than color
I thought the words I spoke passed through your ears and resonated in
your brain and really made you grasp the truth in which I was speaking
Nonetheless
I thought you heard me
Heard my cries and pain and fears
And knowing them
Made you not want to cast the same
I thought your vibe
Passion
Ambition
Blended
Meshed
Intertwined with mine
I thought you knew me

Do Not Pass Go

You were supposed to fight for me
You were supposed to fight for us
For that spark
For that feeling
For our future WE dreamt
For the goals WE set
I gave you an out because you seemed like you wanted one
And no matter how much it hurts me
I will always try and give you what you want
I gave you the get out of jail free card
What we had didn't feel like imprisonment
To me at least
But if you saw it as such then by all means
Here's the key
The only catch is
If you take it
I am no longer the same
I am forever broken
Forever tainted
Forever not knowing what the fuck I'm s'posed to be doing
Yes it means killing me
But I will give it to you anyway
And I'm hoping you don't take it
I'm praying to see you again
I'm wishing this is all one big misunderstanding
I'm SCREAMING for you to CHOOSE ME
STAY WITH ME
BE WITH ME
WORK WITH ME
WE CAN MAKE THIS WORK
WE CAN MAKE IT
And you take it
And my world crumbles
Counted down by the silence of your words I would never hear

You were supposed to rip the card up
Why would you call my peace a prison
What makes you think this is what I want
I'm not going anywhere
I messed up
I'll be better
I focus back in on reality
And I hear a door close
You left
"I appreciate all that you are- and I wish you nothing but the best"
Your last words to me ring ever so faintly in my ear
You left me
"I appreciate all that you are- and I wish you nothing but the best "
What
Ringing
Ringing
How am I gonna get past this
It's like
You leave me lying in the middle of the road
Bleeding
Scraped up
Fractured
And drive off saying "I wish you nothing but the best"
Gee
Thanx

Lucky Stars

I wish I could stop loving you
The way I can turn off a light
I wish your absence didn't make me feel the darkness of being alone
I wish more to eternity that somehow despite it all we could still be
together
And that this pain I have
Would die like the thought of living without you
Secretly
I wish for the impossible
Like your love
Your desire
Your want for me
I wish for time to speed up
So I can see if it is all worth it
If we end up happy
I wish we wanted the same things
I wish my mind never got older
So I could still believe in fairytales
Happily ever afters
Curse breaking kisses
True love
Soulmates
Us
I wish
I wish I could still believe in us

Can We Chill

Life is way too short for this
Can I just be whatever you want me to
Anything you need me to be
Can I just be beside you
No pressure
No expectation
Just take it day by day
One day at a time
Can we just be friends
Get to know each other again
Take things real slow
Talk about nothing
Why can't I just have someone to chill with me
Why don't you want me in your life anymore
I don't want to erase you
I don't want to hate you
I don't want to never speak to you again
Why don't you want me

Still Existing

These are the days
Which I look forward to the least
Surprisingly not the ones where I'm crying so hard I can't get out of bed
But the ones where I miss you so much that I want to speak to you
Because I know
That if something were to happen today
Since tomorrow is never promised
That I would want my last moments to be with you
And I would curse myself for taking that time away
Precious time I could have spent
Loving you
Being in your company
Making new memories
Enjoying you
But yet I was worried bout something that would never happen
And then I start to think if these thoughts even matter
If I'm just being selfish
Why can't I just adapt to the way things are
So everything can go back to the way things were
And I wouldn't have to miss you anymore
I wouldn't have to feel this emptiness
Loneliness
I feel
And some days are good
Where it's okay
Because we're both still existing
Just separately
And I can see myself with someone else
And I can move on
And be happy
And other days it's hard
Because
We're both still existing
Separately

And all I think about is you
And one day coming back to you
And things would be better than it was before
Better than we could ever imagine
And it's that glimmer of hope
That tiny thought that I'm actually waiting for you
That we'll be together again
That our story isn't over
Just paused
Momentarily
That I mean something more to you
And you'll choose me
And realize that your life is better with me in it too
That you know what it feels like when I'm gone
And you don't want to feel that again
That I make you a better you
Like you make me a better me
But until then
I'll just have to survive today
And survive tomorrow
Till it's not surviving anymore
It's living

Worst Day Ever

And just like that
Everything changed
One decision
One night
One moment
I am trying not to be broken
But you pulled my heart from my chest
Like taking clothes out a washer machine
Careless
Thoughtless
Mundane
And I feel the hole in me
My missing piece
Like under my rib cage is so hollow
Empty
I am trying not to miss you
But my everything was you
My person
My love
I felt you through my soul
Cuz you made my soul smile
You made my heart glow
You turned my darkest days into soothing waters with just your presence
You were there for me
You knew me
Better than I thought I needed anyone to
You knew all my faces
The words I would speak before saying them
You knew my pain
You've seen me broken before
You said you loved me and I believed you
You were my person
And yet here you are
Nothing

And every day it's a struggle
And I'm hiding behind a bad bitch mentality
I'm hiding behind anger
Hiding behind lust
I'm miles deep in numbness with my sight set on New Amsterdam
But I am weak
I am broken
I am powerless
To whatever feelings waft over me
Whether my eyes spews gallons of tears
Or are as dry as sand
And still I reminisce
"And I know there's no other place or no other person or no other time or
no other dimension I would rather be in this moment with..."
"My love for you is so fulfilling
That every obstacle that I'm faced with
Is not an obstacle at all
Just a passing rain cloud in the bluest, clearest sky on a perfectly
weathered day"
"That I mean something more to you
And you'll choose me
And realize that your life is better with me in it too
That you know what it feels like when I'm gone
And you don't want to feel that again
That I make you a better you
Like you make me a better me"
And a year ago today was the happiest day of my life
Cuz we finally were official
And today it's the worse

One Less Fairytale

Yes I loved you
But I wasn't in it for the love
I was in it for the laughs
The talks
The friendship
The person I was when I was around you
You challenged me in every way possible
You didn't let me have my way
You corrected me
You comforted me
You opened me up to new ideas
New experiences
You pushed me to strive for more
Want more
To be and do better
I was in it for the moments that happened and was happening
Our moments
For actually pausing to live
I was in it because I could genuinely be myself
With you
Anywhere
I was fearless around you
Yes we had a beautiful future ahead
Or so we thought
But I was in it for the right now
And that was great
That was magical
That was precious
And we gave that all up for what
And it's the hardest thing to get over
To know a dream ended just because you imagined monsters where there
weren't any
Blocked your own path
Held yourself up at gunpoint

I wish true love could die
Like real emotions and real people
But I guess they both kinda just linger
Till enough time passes
Till the heart heals
Till memories and reminders fade away
It's better to have not loved you
To have had one less fairytale
One less dream
One less heartbreak
One less cracked and darkened piece inside of me
It's better to have not loved at all

To The End of My World

I would've followed you to the end of the world
Without looking back
Second thoughts
You being there would've been all the security I needed
As long as we were together
As long as I could still call you mine
And me yours
I would've fought all your battles with you
Side by side
And you knew that
And it burdened you
I loved you that much
I loved you with every inch of me and then some
Time has passed and I can still feel the love I had for you oozing out of
me at times
Like now
I don't understand it you know
Like I can be fine one second
Or for months
Years even
And something brings me back to you
About the time we shared together
And I start thinking about the what ifs
What if we stayed together
What if I never left
What if you took me back
What if we made different decisions
And no matter how I spin it
I don't think I would've been happy today
And I don't think we would still be together today
And knowing this
Knowing it was time to leave
Knowing we did the right thing
Knowing that everything happened for a reason

Knowing that I am happy for the most part
I am still brought to tears
And I still think about you
Wondering how your mom is doing now
If she's ok
If you're ok
If you're happy
And all I can do is hope and pray that you are
And thank you for having more strength than I did at the time
Cuz I would've sacrificed anything for you
Including my happiness
Including my sanity
Including my life

The Real

It's sad
I keep hearing
You should want so much more for yourself
You deserve better
God has something better in store for you
Everything happens for a reason
He wasn't the right one for you
You'll get past this
Niggas ain't shit
You were settling honestly
Love yourself
Focus on yourself
Stop crying
You'll get over it
What are you still sad about
Why don't you have an appetite
Why do you sleep all day
Are you okay
What's wrong
He didn't deserve you
But nobody knows what I know
Nobody felt what I felt with him
We had the best of times
We made each other happy
We didn't have it easy
We lived real lives with real ass problems
Full adulting
But we had each other
And we were there
He was amazing
He was perfect for me
He was good to me
I miss him
I miss everything about him

I miss everything with him
I miss me with him
I miss us
And I'll take the real over fantasy any day
Cuz you made me feel like there should be stories written about our love
I'll take the long hours at work
Cuz I know I would be there when you got home
I'll take you
Cuz you're all I want
You're all I ever want
I can't see myself not loving you
I'm barely living without you
But more than I want this
I want you to want me like this
And that
Is what I shouldn't have to want

The Diamond in The Rough

They say there's always one love that hits detrimentally
One love that differs the way you feel about it
Changes your way of thinking
Your description of normalcy
Your red flags and limitations
And curiously I've been trying to decipher mine
Thinking the more I know myself
The more I compare myself to the before-him and after-him me
The more I am able to locate where the pain is
The more I will be able to understand and disarm my triggers
Then heal
Then love myself better
To in turn love others better
And ultimately being loved better
That was my thought process
Brilliant huh
I mean it sounds like a great plan
But finding out which love burned me the deepest
Scoured my beliefs, my intuition, my judgement
Charred the very edges of my already broken heart
Sifted into the cracks and left nothing but ash, debris, and soot
Is just reliving unimaginable pain
Dwelling in the past
Cuz I never felt so confidently sure that I found the one before
Like things always felt great
And as much as I prayed for situations to work out in the past
There was always a part of me that knew it was a long shot or knew that it
wasn't good for me but it felt good, so I wanted to do it anyway
I was blindsided
And for that I am still trying to forgive myself
But what does any of that matter anyway
I had found my librarian
The diamond in the rough
The which one is not like the others
The good guy
And it turned out
He was a single sequin on the sidewalk that I had happened upon

Not a diamond at all

Now

It's been what
2 and a half years since we broke up
Wow
That long huh
It's been 2 and a half years
Since we broke up
And I still think about you
I still remember the good times we shared
And the things you used to say to me
You know
It's kinda hard to admit
But every time I receive a call from an unknown number
My heart drops a little
Just a fraction of a second
Thinking maybe this could be you coming to your senses
Finally fighting for me
And just that quickly it dissipates
Cuz after 2 and a half years I don't kid myself into thinking that you are
still thinking about me
And honestly, I don't know if I would want to be dating you right now
Even though you miss someone doesn't mean that you should be with
that person
And I get that
And even though you used to love a person doesn't mean you should be
together
And I get that too
But somehow, some way
I figure if I ever get married
You would be the one storming the door to object
And if I had to run into an ex 50 years down the line
I would hope it would be you
And I would hope you lived your life fully and completed everything you
wanted to
I would hope I was always remembered as the one who you let get away

And I would know I was right when I told you our story didn't feel
finished
But what do I know
I can't write how you feel about me
After 2 and a half years
I can very well be forgotten

Tip Of My Tongue

I can still remember what it smelled like walking through your front door
It smelled like the color orange
Something like fall
Airy
Open
It always smelled empty as if you had just moved
As if things were still waiting to be unboxed
Even though I knew you lived there for a long time
Because the bachelor pad decor didn't call for anything other than the
basic necessities
I can still remember your eyes
The way you looked at me
Your small beady eyes
But they glimmered and shined to me
I saw you for the person in front of me
Not who the world made you to be
I can still remember how your lips were
How they felt
You used to lick them often like LL Cool J or something
It was the cutest thing
Thin lips
But the way you kissed me was always so soft and gentle
I remember your laugh
And the different faces you used to make
I remember the way you used to dance around the house
Listening to your music
I remember how you smelled when you just got out the shower
I would play around and want to lick the droplets off your shoulders
And you would laugh and tell me to relax
The way you always wanted to go lay down at the same time
I remember how it felt to lay next to you
How your body felt next to mine

How you used to fight me for the covers because I would always wrap
myself in them
I remember how it felt to hold your hand
You never tried to hurt me
Ever
No test your might
Never playing too rough
I remember the way you used to walk
How you carried yourself
So proud
Defined
Confident
I remember this like if it were yesterday
The last time I was at your crib
The last time I saw you
The last time we spoke
Years ago
I remember it like if it were only moments

Everything I Wish I Could Say to You

Hi
How are you
How have you been
How's your mom and your sister doing
You still at your old place
I miss you sometimes
Do you ever miss me
I know you never meant to hurt me
You taught me so much
Did you really love me
Are you happy
Do you ever wish things would've worked out differently
Do you ever think about her

Not Forgetting You

Trying to forget you
Is like trying to forget the lesson you were sent to deliver me
I realize now
Pushing every emotion that I have ever felt towards you
All my love
Hurt
Passion
And anger
Trying to forget the way you tainted Valentine's Day
The way my heart turned black
The way I released my inner whore to somehow compensate and dilute
my brokenness
Was actually regression
You were in my files to be deleted
I swear every thought you did not consume
Every day that I lived without thinking of you
Without speaking your name
Felt like a victory
A magic eraser to the trail you left behind
And yet
Here I am
Figuring that I was wrong
I can't forget you
Everything has a rhyme a reason
A place
And as tragic as it became
You served your purpose
You were my reminder that I could love again
You were my reminder that I was ready to move on and let go of the past
You were my reminder that no matter how far
 my friends are
They will always be there for me when I need them
And forgetting you
Is forgetting all that I've learned

Invalidating all that I've overcome
Cuz how can you say you weathered the storm
If you don't put the storm in your story
How can you say you reached the peak
If you don't mention the mountain
So welcome back to existence
Don't touch nothing
Don't look at nothing
Don't ask for nothing
I'm over you
Just not forgetting you

The Dark Times: When Depression Strikes

The Hole

It's all around me
Gray
Wet
Cold
Sometimes it's not tall enough to stand up in
Or wide enough to lay down
And sometimes it's the size of a small room
With no corners
Just one wall that reaches infinity and wraps around the whole place
Whether it's made out of stone or anything bad that has ever happened to
me
I don't know
But either way
I find myself picking at it some days
Carving and scratching at the cracks
Hoping it leads to a way out
Or sanity
Some days I pick at it just to keep rhythm
Occupy my time
Focus on something
Some days I feel like my life depends on it
Getting out
But no matter how much I carve, pick, scrape
It all returns to the way it was when I look away
The only proof of me trying
Knowing it was real
Knowing that I was working towards something
Is the blood coming from my hands
The raw feeling of the pads of my fingertips shredding away
The short and missing nails
That stays
The pain always stays

A Seat at The Table

Tired is not even the word
I don't even know the word to be honest
I just don't want to feel like this anymore
I don't like feeling like this
Like I'm the shell of the person I used to be
Like I'm just floating through time and space not really grasping on to
this reality
That's popped up on my screens
I don't know what I feel anymore
Which makes me think
Am I even feeling?
I don't want things to go back to normal because normal was never okay
But I do want to feel like myself again
I do want to be present in my body
I do want to take myself off pause
I do want to know what I want
That's probably the biggest thing for me right now
Knowing what I want and how the fuck to get there
And it's as simple as just sitting down and asking myself
Being a thousand percent honest
And yet
I'm still at the table
Waiting for an answer
Willing for it to hit me
Praying for guidance
Hoping for something
It's a different kind of numb
Different kind of empty
Yep

The Greatest Act of All Time

One thing I don't like
Being vulnerable for too long
I can have my moments
As should everyone
But being vulnerable for too long
Hurting in view for too long
Showing how much I am concerned
Feeling like I've done my all but it's still not enough
Pushing and fighting and at the same time not moving at all
Praying and supporting and failing
Staying safe and staying compliant
Seeing myself utilizing my coping methods
Staying busy
Being lustful
Refocusing my attention
Checking on everyone but myself
Not realizing until being still
That I am magnificently displaying the biggest distraction I have seen to
date
That my sweet mind is on autopilot and it is trying to save me
Preserve my happiness
Preserve my loving and giving soul
Preserve my empathetic nature that allows me to feel for people I do not
know
Mourn for people I have not lost
I didn't know that I was still in pain
I see that I have reached a new level of disguising it even from myself
The peak of crying silently
Not crying at all

What Is It?

It's the sadness
The darkness
The hole
The sinking feeling
It's being so far in your bed that you feel under it
It's the never being able to climb out
The hopelessness
The nobody understands
The isolation
Separation
It's the worthlessness
The disappointment
The weight on your shoulders
Feeling heavy all the time
Like gravity has zeroed in on your body and maximized itself to holding
you down
It's the pressure
The pain you'll cause others if they knew your pain
It's the peace that you think you will feel
When it's all over
The rest
The not having to fight anymore
The final sleep to being so damn tired all the time
It's knowing that even in your peace others won't get it
That you'll end up hurting the people you love
And either way it seems like a lose-lose situation
But you're picking yourself
Because you matter too
And you deserve to be selfish with your life
It's the crying
Debating
Talks with God
The many decisions left up to you that are all overwhelming

It's the silence around you
The hearing your own breathing
The sniffling of snot as your nose starts to clog and run at the same time
And for whatever reason you choose, you put the pills back on the dresser
Not tonight you say
Not tonight

The Fighting Times: Being Black In America

America

I'm not your superwoman
My pain is real
I bleed red just like you
My bruises are blue just like yours
My soul is pure
It's my red pouring onto that flag
Spilling from the cuts of my ancestors
Seeping from the lashes of today
Quenching the thirst of hateful, bigoted, evil beings
Watching it drip for sick amusement
Thinking that I don't feel it
My pain is real
The darkest of blues
Brought to the surface of my skin by nightsticks in the hands of my so-called protectors
Thinking their liberation can only be funded by my incarceration
That their voices can only be heard when mine is dead silent
That anger and retaliation is a one-way street
That my success acquired from the second-handed scraps of education,
job-opportunities, and poorly funded environment that is "blessed' upon
me is a danger and threat to their way of living
My pain is real
It's my soul
That prevails through their wicked ways
My soul that has the capacity to want love and equality
My soul that emanates the angelic voices that have the power to move us
The creativity that demonstrates our expression
The rhythm and magic that stirs within us
Clean
Pure
White
So if you ask me
I am America
I'm the red, white, and blue hanging at full mast

Shit I'm more American than you
And know if you tryna burn me down
America bout to burn down too

Jealous Much

I'm curious
Help me understand this
If you will
What gives you the right
To put me in shackles and handcuffs
And call me the bad guy
When you're the one committing all the crimes
Killing all our leaders and great thinkers
Shooting our men, women, and children
Lynching our great grandparents and our future
Stealing our money, ideas, and bodies
Ripping us off
Benefitting off us
Profiting off us
Living off us and our labor
Collecting the sweat off our backs and trickling them on your forehead
talking bout
"Phew that was some hard work
Boy, I'm tired
I think I need to take a break"
Seriously
You laugh and mock us when we tell you to stop belittling us
Stop calling us one name
Stop portraying us as wild savages, gangsters, crack fiends and the help
But then you are outraged when we make our own depictions of
ourselves as kings, queens, superheroes, and doctors
There's no such thing as "too white"
But "too black" is deemed ghetto, urban, or anything more than the one
token best friend role in a movie
You compare your oppression of having to wait in line at Starbucks for
your morning coffee like everyone else
To our regulatory traffic stop at the end of the month for doing nothing
wrong but driving while black
That can either end in a 20 min hold up, brutal arrest, or death

You steal our culture and strip us from our history
And when we savor, re-write, or create something new
You steal that too and call yourselves the originators
What is it inside of you that makes you so extremely fascinated yet
horrifically destructive when it comes to black people
You love us when we are playing sports or entertaining you
But hate us when we live beside you
Tell me how that makes sense
You clown us for the way God shaped us
But you pay thousands of dollars to be shaped just like that
My hair can do everything your hair can do
But your hair can't do everything my hair can do
But you not only say that you have the better hair type
I also have to cover my hair to look like yours
Or change my hair to look like yours
So it can be accepted and okay to have
I mean the list goes on and on
We can be here for days
I just wanna know with all this
Like honestly why are you mad though
It sounds like jealousy to me
But like damn how long does jealousy last
And do you even recognize it as such
I'm just curious

My Black Men

My black men
This is why I love yall like I do
Why I give yall so much of me
Why I believe in your dreams
Why I hold you at night
Why I satisfy your hunger
Why I seek to give you pleasure
My black men
You are beautiful beyond this world can measure
You are stronger than minds can comprehend
You are uniquely created
My black men
I will never stop loving you
I will never give up on you
I see your light
I feel your pain
I see in the depth of your eyes
The scream you are constantly trying to mask
All the built-up words you have nowhere to express
No podium to stand on
No listening ears
I see the tiredness
The fear
The anger
The sadness
The confusion
Why do they hate us so much
Why won't they let us live
I hear you my black men
I see you my black men
I appreciate you my black men
I am with you my black men
I will fight beside you my black men

Wakey Wakey

ALL BLACK PEOPLE DO NOT OWN GUNS!!!!
WHAT YOU'RE SEEING IS MY SKIN
THE SKIN I WAS BORN IN
NOT THE SKIN I CHOSE TO WEAR TODAY
NOT THE SKIN THAT IS REQUIRED TO IDENTIFY MYSELF AT
MY JOB
NOT THE SKIN I GET PAID TO BE IN
NOT THE SKIN I CAN TAKE OFF AT ANY GIVEN TIME
NOT THE SKIN THAT MADE ME TAKE AN OATH TO SERVE
AND PROTECT PEOPLE
NOT THE SKIN THAT I ASKED GOD FOR
NOT THE SKIN THAT I ASKED MY PARENTS FOR
THE SKIN
I
LIKE YOU
AND EVERY OTHER LIVING THING IN THIS WORLD
HAD UTTERLY AND COMPLETELY LACK OF CONTROL IN
WAS BORN WITH
NOW
IF MY HANDS ARE UP
IF MY BACK IS TURNED
IF I AM LYING FACE DOWN ON MY STOMACH IN HANDCUFFS
IF I AM SHIELDING MY FACE FROM THE BLOWS OF YOUR
FOOT
IF I AM HOLDING MY RIBS THAT YOU BROKE
IF I AM UNBUCKLING THE SEATBELT YOU JUST YELLED AT
ME TO REMOVE
FOR FUCK'S SAKE
I AM NOT REACHING FOR A GUN!!!
I AM IN FEAR OF MY LIFE
BECAUSE THE JUSTIFICATION FOR MY MURDER WILL
ALWAYS BE THAT YOU FEARED FOR YOUR LIFE
LIKE YOU ARE THE ONLY ONE WHO IS ALLOWED TO BE
SCARED

LIKE YOU'RE THE ONE WHO IS BREATHING YOUR LAST
BREATH WHILE YOU DELIBERATELY ARE DRAINING MINE
LIKE I SOUGHT YOU OUT
AND APPROACHED YOU
I AM AFRAID 24 HOURS A DAY
7 DAYS A WEEK
THERE IS NO PLACE THAT'S SAFE
NOT EVEN IN MY OWN HOME
NOT EVEN IN BED IN THE ARMS OF THE MAN I LOVE
TELL ME
HOW THE FUCK AM I SUPPOSED TO LIVE
Right
Mhmm
I see
Well, when you're able to go home at night
Take off your uniform
Kiss the people you love
And fall asleep without a care in the world
I hope you wake up black

At The End of The Tunnel

I hope you have realized how amazingly brilliant you are
I hope all the history and knowledge you have been receiving
Gave you that self-justification
That you have and always will be beautiful beyond compare
I hope you seen that you are loved by so many
That your rights are worth fighting for
Your life is worth fighting for
I hope you understand the magnitude of what we can do when we stand together
I hope you are living the best life you possibly can in spite of everything else
I hope you allow yourself to feel happiness
And peace
And hold on to that light inside you
I hope this message reaches you with all the love and positivity my soul can exert
Stay strong my people

The High Times:
Being High

High Thoughts Pt. 1

I want to write down all my high thoughts
There should be a book of high thoughts
Bupitta bupitta
Alyson and Cinderella
I want to spell children like children
Cinderella like children is what I was trying to say
Bupitta bupitta
Yo that book is a great idea
We rich biotch
My shoulder is hot
I have no eyebrows
Where are my eyebrows
Everyone else has eyebrows
My hand is like a claw
Heavy hand
I can't stop nodding
The high comes in waves
Ocean sounds
Hold the boobs
This is the greatest idea ever
You're a hot dog in a hat with a green flag
You walk around like I'm the shit when you lowkey the shit cuz you not
all about being the shit you like well if nobody thinks I'm the shit than I
think I'm the shit cuz why can't I be the shit so Imma walk around like
I'm the shit
My mouth feels weird
Like metal
You slapped the high out of me
For a good 5 seconds 5 seconds secure
Sober*
I'm dead trying to remember who did that shit so I cannot like them more

High Thoughts Pt. 2

I was the wicked witch of the west
Screaming I'm melting I'm melting
Cotton mouth like a bitchhhh
My toes are maaaaaaaaaddddd ashy and omg he keeps bumping into
them
I keep curling once I start
I'm high afffffff
I am not seeing colors
Have to explain my love language
I'm sooooo moving in slow motion
As slow as a sloth
I hope I am writing in English
This looks like English
I hope this makes sense
I have to pee

The Clearest Times: Motivation

All The Right People

My smile has gotten brighter
My laugh
Louder
My decisions
More intentional
My mistakes
More forgiving
My wants
Bolder
Fearful
Met
I am loving myself a little more these days
And the results are amazing
I don't have everything figured out
And it's depressing some days and liberating the next
But each moment I spend by myself
Is more clarifying and honest
I am figuring out exactly what I want and don't want
I am living my life exactly how I choose to
I am building stronger bonds with my family and friends that have
always been there for me
Time that I usually dedicate to a significant other
Time that I spend fantasizing or healing from heartbreak
All this extra time now dedicated to people that deserve it
And even that action
Making sure the people I love know that
Is a wonderful feeling in itself
I may be single
But I'm loving all the right people right now

Bars

Not even a revenge body
Better me body
Do for me body
I'm on fleek body
Happy me body

Clarity

I miss you
But I don't need you
It's nice having you though
I miss us talking
But it feels nice to not always have to be by my phone

How Lessons Pt. 5 Should've Went

Play
And I tried to back off
I tried to give you space
Trust me when I say
I tried to take things slow
But I feel like your actions are not taking it slow with me
The only thing you're slow with is saying you're committed to me
Pause
Because he doesn't want to be committed to you
People know what they want
He's gonna take all that he can from you for as long as you let him
And he'll say whatever he needs to
And do whatever he needs to
To keep up his facade
But babygirl, it is indeed a facade
But continue
Play
Because you tell me that you're not interested in anyone else
Pause
He's lying
That's what you want to hear
Sounds nice huh
Makes you feel special
Uh huh
He knows
That's what he tells the others too
Play
So you basically already are
Pause
HA
Basically not
You're playing yourself right now
Play
And I don't know what else you're not doing now
That you would be doing if we were together
Pause
Sis this ain't it

For one telling the truth
Two actually caring about you
But it's okay
It's a real fucked up lesson you're learning with this one
But I guess it necessary or whatever
Play
I mean you are the one saying things like
"When you're my wife"
And seeing us with no kids
And talking about a far, far future
Pause
Because that's what you want to hear
Play
That's not taking it slow
That doesn't make me feel like we're taking it slow
And how am I just supposed to be normal with that
Or not be attached to you
I just don't understand
Pause
Because it's bullshit
And you're not supposed to
It doesn't make sense
Play
And yes everything is fine
Pause
Girl what
How is this fine
Play
Nothing is wrong
Pause
Um excuse me what
Everything is wrong
What are you seeing that is right
He's playing you hard body
Run girl
Run, run, as fast as you can
He's creeping and lying, he ain't a good man
Play
But this isn't the first time this has come up
Pause
Cuz you're smart

You know you get that feeling in your gut
But you rather focus on all the good feelings instead
Trust your gut mama
It's never wrong
Play
And I'm only addressing it because it still bothers me
I thought we were going somewhere
That you were maybe catching up
That's all
But if you still want me to slow down
I'll try
End
You don't need to try
He's not gonna catch up
Cuz he doesn't want to
Leave him alone
He's not at all what you think and at all what you need
You deserve so much more than what he is giving you
You are smart, and talented, and beautiful, and giving, and ambitious, and genuine
He could never match up to a 5th of the being you are
You are incredible
You are light itself
You are blessed and highly favored
You don't have to settle
And if he doesn't respect your feelings the first time you acknowledge them, then there is nothing there for you baby
It's okay though
I know you are a loving person and are just being you
You're doing your best
And you're learning
Trust me it gets better
I love you girl

<u>Yes</u>

As her lips curve like the mountain tops
And the arcs in her brows form like the deepest caves
The slope of her nose mirrors that of the hills
Her skin
Smooth as the ocean flowing over stone

It's Not Your Fault

You can't even be mad that you trusted him
Utterly
Fully
Completely
That yes you had some doubts here and there
From a small state of jealousy or insecurity
But at the end of the day, it was always "You're being crazy"
He proved himself to you over and again
And you believed him
And it's not your fault
He did nothing wrong
Until he did
He earned your trust
And then lost it
And it's okay
Cuz you were to trust him until you couldn't anymore
Because everything dies
Colors fade
Seasons change
Time goes on
Just breathe through it
Breathe
Inhale
Through
Exhale
It
Cuz you will get through this
Like you've gone through the ones in the past
You'll just have to fight a little harder
Cuz the wound is deeper
And it hurts a lot more
But you will heal
Your soul won't cry anymore
You will move on

You will be happy again
You will keep telling yourself it is not your fault until you believe it
Every time
Not just sometimes
It is not your fault
It was okay to trust him
Until you couldn't anymore
Everything comes to an end
Time goes on
And you will grieve how you choose fit
Because you did lose something
And however you need to express and accept that is okay
You will be okay
I love you

Everyone is doing the best they can
People are going to make mistakes
Simply because they have never been where they are before
And if they have then it's a choice
Don't take it personal
Do what's best for you

Picasso Nigga

Yo real talk
There's no way I'm not getting it
My dreams are deadass mine
The way my dopeness transforms
From a thought created in my mind
To a complete and utter masterpiece
Is like the revealing of a Picasso
It just is nigga

Thank Me

I understand that everything happened for a reason
Even if I don't see it now
It somehow made me a better person
Because I am better than I was before
Because every day I strive to be better than I was the day before
Everyday leads me one step closer to being the person that I know I can be
And I am here despite my tragedies
I have fought through my weaknesses
I have triumphed over my fears
I lit my own path
Whether I had the light from the sun or the light from a matchstick
I made it here
So thank me
I did it
And I am damn proud

About The Author

Born and raised in Queens, New York, Dominique Dorsey finally releases her debut book *Still Existing*. As an empath and the epitome of a cancer woman, she uses her personal experiences of never being understood to connect with young adults suffering from heartbreak, depression, and loneliness. From being bullied as a child to getting dumped on Valentine's Day, this hopeless romantic shares her most vulnerable thoughts in hopes of inspiring others to live through the good and bad days. Dominique continues to write poetry as well as embarking on a new journey of writing a self-help book. When she is not expressing her emotions through words, you can find her expressing her emotions through movement as a choreographer in Miami.

Made in the USA
Columbia, SC
03 February 2024

31389571R00072